SEEK TO TRUST

SEEKING IN ROMANCE BOOK 5

KEKE RENÉE

304 PUBLISHING COMPANY

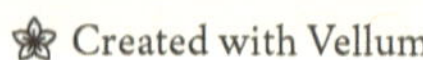 Created with Vellum

LATEST RELEASES BY KEKE RENÉE:

- Wet Heat (Wet Heat Series Book 1)
- Every Time We Touch Novelette (Wet Heat Book 2 Series)
- His Peace, Her Pleasure
- Baby, It's Cold Outside
- Love Don't Live Here Anymore, Vanessa Andrew Book 1
- Love Don't Live Here Anymore, Isabella Andrew Book2
- One Night Only-A Novelette (Love By Design Book 1)
- Cassian and Savannah (Love By Design Book 2)
- Deidra's Love (Love By Design Book 3)
- Protecting Bria (Special Force Operation Alphas)
- Sensual
- Seek To Please Book 1
- Seek To Touch Book 2
- Seek To Bare Book 3
- Seek To Love Book 4

• Protecting Chanel (Special Forces Operation Alphas)
• Seek To Trust Book 5

I WANT TO THANK first my readers for loving these characters so much and waited so love for them to come back.

ACKNOWLEDGMENTS

I CAN'T MENTION ENOUGH the support and dedication of my author buddies for keeping me uplifted. My behind-the-scenes team of beta readers, editors, designers, and more. As a writer I continue to strive for the best, and I appreciate everyone who reads my work. Without your continual feedback, I wouldn't be on this path, letting doubts slip away.

INTRODUCTION

Are you signed up for my newsletter?

Join today and find out all the latest in new releases, contests, giveaways, sneak peeks, and more.

https://BookHip.com/BKRPJL

DISCLAIMER

THIS WORK OF FICTION contains strong language and explicit sexual content and is only intended for mature readers. This story may contain unconventional situations, language, and sexual encounters that may offend some readers. This book is for mature readers (18+).

SYNOPSIS

Emma's been happily in love with Jordan most of her life. Now, as parents to a little boy and working on her business, she's finding Jordan is spending less and less time with her as he navigates his family's business. Being his wife and his sister's best friend, Emma wonders if she made the wrong decision when her trust is broken.

CHAPTER 1

EMMA

"I hope you're enjoying yourself. I can't believe you, Jordan." I dropped my phone on the table, glanced around the food I made, and blew out the candles. Today was supposed to be about us reconnecting and making time for our relationship. He promised he would come home straight away, but once again, he lied. Jordan was a busy man, working for his family's business, but today was about his marriage. Chelsey was cool with watching our son tonight, which made my plans complete. Everyone knew I had the evening blocked off and not to disturb us unless it was an emergency with our son.

Since I became a mom, all of my time was focused on him and trying to stay on top of work. Jordan and I barely spoke to each other unless it was about our child. Our life was a routine of us getting up in the morning, getting dressed, and leaving for the day. No more breakfast dates or weekend getaways for just the two of us. We'd been together for a while, and I knew some marriages grew stagnant, but I never saw myself being one of those couples.

I lifted the plate of food, walked into the kitchen, and dumped it in the trash; it wasn't even worth saving. He loved when I made marinated chicken, greens, baked potato, and spaghetti. Even his favorite dessert of strawberry shortcake would have been presented before we headed upstairs to the bedroom. Not up for washing dishes, I placed the leftovers in the fridge and grabbed my cell to march upstairs and turn on the shower. I scrolled through social media and saw he posted a photo of him with his coworkers out at a bar.

"That bastard," I hissed, put my phone on the counter, turned the shower up to the highest temperature, and removed my cocktail dress. Sliding the door open, I stepped in to reach for the towel and lemon body wash. I still remembered the day we met when I picked him up from the airport. We just hit it off from there. He was used to women falling over his charm, and I set him straight out the gate that I wasn't like most women. Now almost five years later we'd been together, and things slowed down since our son.

"He really went out with me," I hissed, dropping the bottle of lotion on the nightstand, slipped under the covers, and took a screenshot of social media before turning my phone off.

"Mmmmmm..." My eyes slowly flickered open when I felt kisses trail along my thigh.

"You smell so good, baby." Jordan groaned and rubbed my stomach. Finally focused on what he was doing, I slapped his hand away.

"What the fuck, Emma?"

"Leave me alone, Jordan." I turned my back to him and pushed my gown down.

"What's wrong with you?" His hand reached around to pull my chin toward him.

"Go to sleep or better yet, go back to your friends." I pushed his hand away and peered at the clock. It was three in the morning.

"Baby."

"Go to sleep, Jordan."

He groaned, fumbled around, and rose out of bed. I fell back asleep and planned to ignore him.

* * *

THE NEXT MORNING, I poured the coffee in my cup and stared at the news program discussing the weather updates and reached for a piece of bacon. I stood at the island and wiped my hands when he stalked in and wrapped his arms around my waist.

"Morning, beautiful."

"Hey."

He dropped his hand, then turned me to face him.

"What did I do?"

In irritation, I twitched my nose

"Jordan, leave me alone please."

"Woman, I'm not dealing with the silent treatment all day." He reached for a coffee cup and poured himself a coffee. He looked around the stove and then me.

"You didn't cook me breakfast?"

"No."

"Emma, you're being petty."

I scoffed and bit into my toast in front of his face.

"Are you going to tell me what I did wrong?"

"What happened yesterday, Jordan?"

"What do you mean?"

"That's why you're getting the silent treatment." I trashed the rest of my bacon and eggs and finished my coffee before walking out of the kitchen. For him not to remember what yesterday meant for us as a couple hurt, and I didn't know what he had going on, but he needed to get his act together before I decided to leave.

* * *

HOURS LATER, I clocked out for lunch and knocked on Chelsey's door and waited for her to respond.

"The door is open."

I pushed it forward and smiled at her behind her desk. She'd taken on the role of manager of this branch and collaborated with her brother. The Hayden family was well known in Memphis, and I was surprised they didn't hold resentment the way they did with her husband, Xavier, after they made things official.

"Hey, sis." I sat on the couch in her office.

"Are you headed to lunch?"

I nodded and picked up the magazine on the table.

"Yep, are you coming?"

"Sure. I was waiting on Xavier, but I think he's held up with work."

"How was my baby last night?"

"Great as usual."

"I'll grab him when I leave here today."

"You don't have to. He loves staying with his aunt and uncle."

I laughed because we both knew they spoiled him with his own room at their place. Anything he wanted, they gave to him. I had to fuss with Xavier to not buy him more toys whenever they went out of town.

"You two spoil him so much." I leaned my head against the couch with my hand resting on its side.

"He deserves it though." Chelsey turned her computer off and reached for her purse and jacket.

"Between you and your parents, my baby will never have to lift a finger."

"Especially with my parents. Lily told me that my parents set up his own room, plus a playroom."

"He doesn't even have a playroom at home." I threw my hands up in surrender.

Chelsey laughed, and I jumped up to head out of her office.

"Where are we going today?" She tucked her hand in her jacket.

"Thinking about pizza."

Chelsey and I headed out of the bank to the local pizza joint around the corner.

CHAPTER 2

JORDAN

"Fuck!" I slammed the phone on my desk after Emma ignored my call for the fourth time. Once I checked my calendar, I saw I had last night blocked out for Emma. It was supposed to be dinner just the two of us, and I fucked up big time. I prayed she would forgive me. Last night wasn't purposely missed. I truly hoped she would let me make it up to her today. I would have my assistant schedule a getaway trip if she was free from the bank.

Knock! Knock!

"Mr. Hayden." My assistant stepped in my office.

"Yeah, Capri."

"Miss Asha is here."

I rubbed my forehead and sat back in my seat. Asha Knight was one of our biggest clients at the bank, and we'd done a lot of work with them over the years. Asha was a princess, and her father handed over most of his business to her. They were looking into buying a few properties. We not only had our family business in banking, but real estate as well. Signing a major deal with the Knight family would be huge for the city and us as the premier business for other corporations.

"Send her in, Capri."

The biggest problem with Asha was she wanted everything when she wanted it and fuck anyone else who refused.

She slid the door open further. Asha removed her shades and swished her hips into my office and smiled. Asha had a problem with flirting and not understanding we would never be an item.

"Have a seat, Asha." I motioned to the chair in front of me.

"No morning hug, Jordan?" Asha removed her coat and like I thought, she wore the skimpiest skirt with a slit on the side. Her breasts spilled over her white blouse. All she did was try to get my attention, and I laughed at her too many times to even care.

"Asha, how are you?" I extended a hand to keep it business related.

She didn't like my gesture with the weak shake she gave me.

"I was good until I heard you were thinking of putting someone else in charge of this deal."

"You have to understand, Asha, as the CEO of the company, I need to delegate certain deals."

"I have no doubt, but I only want you to handle me." Asha hovered over my desk, with her breasts right in my face. I peered from her eyes, down to her chest, and then her eyes again.

"See something you like?" she asked, and I cleared my throat.

Knock! Knock!

"Yeah, Capri."

"Sorry, sir. I have your mother here with your son." Capri stood at the door.

"I thought he was with my sister?" I jumped up. Asha stood and buttoned the rest of her blouse.

"She didn't want to disturb you, but Emma hadn't picked up her call," Capri explained, and I whipped my head toward Asha. Somehow, she and Emma didn't get along. Many times, I had to divert them running into each other, so the deal didn't fall through.

"Send them in, and I'll try Emma again." I grabbed my cell and dialed her number.

"*This is Emma Hayden. I can't get to the phone right now—*" I ended the voicemail and dropped my phone on the desk. My mom stepped into my office and smiled at Asha. I took Jr. out of her hands. He was two years old and looked exactly like me, with a little of Emma's features. I wanted more kids to give my son siblings like I had growing up.

"Hey, Mom."

"Hi, baby. Asha, I haven't seen you in so long." Mom extended her arm out for a hug.

"Mrs. Hayden, good to see you. Is this your little guy?" Asha pinched Jr.'s cheek, and he pushed her hand away. Asha was embarrassed, and I laughed as my mom corrected him.

"What are you doing up here?" I sat him on my lap.

"Emma didn't pick up my call, and I thought I would come here and drop him off."

"She's probably in a meeting."

"If I didn't have this charity meeting, I would have kept him longer. Daycare center said he wasn't feeling well."

I placed a hand on his forehead. It felt warm.

"Thanks for grabbing him," I said.

"No problem, son. Tell Emma to call me later."

"She's not talking to me right now."

"Why? You know what? Keep me out of this."

I learned from Chelsey and Xavier that it was safer to stay away from my sister's drama with my parents, and I did the same for me and Emma. Even though my parents came around to the idea of Xavier as her husband, it was a hard journey. Both of them could be judgmental, and Emma had it rough at the beginning, not only from me, but my parents when we officially started dating.

"Emma will call you later." She walked out of my office.

"So, I take it our meeting is over?" Asha asked, planting her hand on her hips.

"Yeah, sorry. I need to get my son home."

"You know if you ever need any help with him…"

"Asha." I groaned at her attempt to flirt in front of my son.

"All I'm saying to you, Jordan, is that you used to be happy." She winked, slid her black shades on, and lifted her jacket before strolling out of my office. Jr. laid his head on my chest, and I blew out a breath and thought of how I could fix things with Emma. I knew I was fighting a losing battle the moment she spoke when I first met her; she owned my heart. As short as she was, her confidence and brains pulled me.

"Are you ready to go see Mommy?" I asked, and he picked his head up and looked at me.

"I knew you were faking." I chuckled, and he giggled, falling back on my chest.

* * *

I UNLOCKED THE DOOR, carried Jr. on my shoulder and his backpack on my arm, and noticed Emma on the couch in sweatpants and her hair up in a ponytail.

"How long have you been here?" I placed Jr. on the

loveseat opposite her.

"An hour, why?"

"Your son is sick. You didn't think to call me back?"

"Why didn't you leave a message?" Emma put her glass of wine down, grabbed Jr. from the loveseat, and rubbed his stomach.

"Baby, you sick?" He slowly nodded his head, wrapping his arms around her neck.

"All right, you want to play games." I tossed my jacket on the couch and put his backpack on the floor.

"Jordan, you have the nerve to come at me. After what you did." She hissed.

"Emma, I messed up. Sorry I missed our dinner." I squatted down in front of her.

"Okay."

"Okay? That's all I get?"

"Okay is not what you deserve, but since my son is right here, I want to keep it about him." She popped her lips.

I knew this was a losing battle, so I walked into the kitchen and saw she had prepared dinner. I was grateful she even thought of me since I barely ate breakfast. Once I fixed a plate, I came out of the kitchen and saw she was gone, but the TV was still on. After I plopped down on the couch with the beer, she came back in with a pair of black tights and my white shirt. She rolled her eyes, and I smirked when she sat next to me on the couch.

"Baby, this food is good."

"It should be; it was left over from last night."

"Can you forgive me please? I'll do anything to get out of the doghouse." I put everything on the table, turned toward her, and caressed her thigh.

"I forgive you, Jordan. I'm just disappointed."

"Understandable."

"When did we become these people?"

"What people?" My brow bent in confusion.

"Roommates."

"All right, Emma, you're crazy. I'm not your fucking roommate." I gripped her chin.

She pushed my hand away.

"Could have fooled me. You used to be up under me all the time, and now it's like I can barely get a phone call from you."

"I have been a little extra busy."

"A little, Jordan?"

"Marriage is a two-way commitment. You've been missing in action."

"What is that supposed to mean?"

"When was the last time you sucked my dick?"

"Fuck you, Jordan." She jumped up, and I reached for her hand. She pushed me away and stormed off.

"Emma! Emma!"

The bedroom door slammed shut, and Jr. started to cry.

"Fuck, man." I checked on Jr. and rubbed his stomach to put him back to sleep. I came out of his room and glanced at our bedroom. I heard sniffles and tapped on the bedroom door.

"Please leave me alone, Jordan."

"Baby, let me talk to you." I felt like shit.

Ring! Ring!

"Hello."

I heard Emma answer the phone, but when I twisted the doorknob, it was locked.

"Really? She locked me out," I muttered to myself.

"Yeah, hold on," I heard Emma say. A second later, the door jerked open, and the expression on her face told me she was ready to kick my ass.

"Who's on the phone?" I asked.

"Your client Asha Knight. I guess you forgot your wallet last night." Emma shoved the phone in my chest and slammed the door again, which caused Jr. to cry again.

"Shit! This is Jordan Hayden." I forgot Asha showed up at the bar last night. We'd celebrated closing another deal, and she popped up. I forgot to even stop off at the bar that we went to because I wanted to get my son home. A few of my employees dropped me off, and I climbed into bed horny and ready to fuck my wife.

"Jordan, I have something you want." Asha snickered over the phone.

"Asha, you could have left my wallet at the office this morning."

"Oops. I forgot."

"Yeah."

"Don't be mad. I'll bring it to you now."

"Ugh, no that's not going to work."

"Why not?"

"Because I'm home, and you're a client."

"Jordan, you worry too much. Who answered your phone? Was that Capri?"

"Asha, I don't have time right now to get into a long conversation."

"Jordan, you seem stressed. Maybe I could take you out for dinner."

The bedroom door swung open, and Emma glared at me.

"You're seriously on the phone with another woman, Jordan. Get out of my way before I slap you."

She tried to walk around me, but I blocked her and grasped her waist.

"Asha, I'll have Capri schedule a meeting to discuss the building permits." Emma tried to push me back, but I tightened my hold and buried my face in her neck.

"Are you listening to me—" I ended the call before Asha could continue.

"That was a client." I rubbed her back.

"Could have fooled me." She avoided my eyes and crossed her hands over her chest.

"Come have dinner with me so we can talk."

"Not hungry."

"I apologize for missing our dinner. It'll never happen again. Also, I apologize for the comment I made. You're the most important person to me."

"Maybe we should do counseling."

"Have we gotten that far off the rails? Ignoring calls and counseling."

"Honestly, you've changed."

"How?" I let my hands fall.

"You're never here and when you are, it's to hang with Jr."

"You have to admit some fault, Emma. All you do is hang with Jr. or Chelsey."

She ran a hand through her hair and nodded.

"You might be right."

I captured her lips and sucked on her tongue.

"We both need to do better in this marriage."

"I agree, but you need to get your clients in check and tell them not to call here after five."

"That won't happen again."

"What did you do last night?"

"A few of the employees took me to the bar, and we celebrated a deal. I lost track of time and my brain cells."

"You did."

"Let's go to the living room and finish this movie."

"Our conversation is not over, Jordan."

"Didn't say it was, dear."

CHAPTER 3

EMMA

*J*r. ran fast to his friends in daycare, and I smiled looking at my little boy for how well I'd been able to transition to becoming a mom after many years of being single. I never thought I would be someone's mom. He slept through the night, didn't give us too many problems, and never cried at every moment. He was extremely quiet and thought before he did anything. Jordan and I were so blessed.

"He looks better." Sloan, his teacher, approached me.

"Yeah, I just kept him home, away from other kids, and let him rest."

"No need to worry. I think you're doing a great job." Sloan patted me on the shoulder.

"Thanks. Here's his backpack with his favorite book and food."

Sloan took the bag, and I turned to leave. I checked my watch and saw I had a few hours before I needed to meet the girls for lunch. I arrived at work and saw Jordan outside with a client. The way she leaned into him shot my anxiety high. I opened the door, slammed it shut, strolled over, and stood next to him.

"Hello, I'm Mrs. Hayden." I stuck my hand out.

Her lips turned up in disgust.

"Asha Knight, a client and partner of Jordan's."

"Partner?" My brow hiked at her statement.

She smirked. Jordan pulled me back behind him.

"Asha, I'll be in touch."

"Please call me when you decide, no matter the time." Asha winked at him, and I balled my fists up.

Jordan turned to me, and I glared at him and cocked my head to the side.

"Baby, it was a business meeting."

"Is she the one who called you that night?" I would be a widow real soon and find Jr. another father, depending on his lie.

He ran a hand down his head.

"Yeah, baby, it's only business."

"Did you sleep with her?"

"Emma, stop being stupid."

"Fuck you, Jordan." I stormed off, ran into the building, and stomped to my office. Chelsey was laughing with a coworker.

"Hey, Emma!" Chelsey waved, and I motioned with my hand up.

"Emma! Emma!" Jordan screamed behind me.

I slammed my office door and paced back and forth to calm my nerves.

"Will you calm down?" Jordan shut and locked my door.

"Get out." I grimaced, removed my coat, and walked around my desk, pulling the chair up.

"No."

I pointed my finger at him.

"If you want her, then fuck her."

"What are you talking about? I love you."

"Since when? You promised to make some changes, and I haven't seen anything."

"What can I do to show you I want you and only you?"

I scoffed and turned my chair around to look out of my window at the traffic.

He shifted my chair around, reached for my hands, and pulled me into his arms.

"I want you, only you. Asha doesn't mean anything to me."

"Jordan, move." I tried to push him away, but he didn't move.

"I want you to take the rest of the day off. Get your hair and nails done."

"Why? I have too much work here." I glanced at the pile of paperwork on my desk.

"That can wait. Take Chelsey with you."

"Jordan, if you're trying to get alone time with your girlfriend, you don't need me out of the way."

He slammed me on the ass.

"Shut up. Asha doesn't mean shit to me. I was telling her I moved her deal to another business manager."

"You did?"

"Yes, give me a chance to make this right." He started to trail kisses down my cheek and behind my ear.

"Well," I cooed, grasping him around the neck.

"I promise my life is you and Jr."

"Okay."

He slid his hand in his pocket, pulled out two hundred dollars, and placed it in my hand.

"Tonight, I'm taking you to the club."

"Seriously?"

"It's been a while, and we haven't played since Jr. arrived." He grinned and gripped both of my ass cheeks.

"Thank you, baby."

"You'll be thanking me later tonight."

"You think you know me." I laughed and slammed his chest lightly.

* * *

THE MASSAGE WAS the best I'd had in a long time, and I couldn't wait to have Jordan's hands all over me. After our argument, I caught up on a little work and then left to come to the spa; Chelsey tagged along, and we met Maya here.

"So, she was in his face when you pulled up?" Chelsey wondered, finished with her massage.

"Yes, and I held my composure because I could feel myself ready to snatch her dusty wig off."

Chelsey giggled, and I rolled my eyes.

"That girl has beautiful hair," Chelsey said.

"So, whose side are you on?" I lifted up and tightened the towel around my body.

"Always on your side, boo. I knew something was wrong when you just walked by me earlier."

I slid my feet into my sandals and walked out of the room to re-dress and get our nails done.

"I was so heated. Maya, how are things with you and Mason?" She opened the door to the dressing room.

"Nice, we're doing good. I had a few days off from the senate this week, and Mason took time off with me," Maya explained.

"See, your husband makes you a priority. I can barely get mine to have dinner." I could feel my annoyance heighten.

"Relax, Emma. You're having dinner with him tonight, right?"

"Yes." I pouted, taking out my jogging pants and shirt to re-dress.

"Then give him a chance to get better. I know Jordan, and when he knows you're hurt, he'll spend the rest of the day or week trying to make up for his mistakes," Chelsey said.

I nodded and slid my purse out of the locker.

We strolled to the nail section, and they had our seats lined up for our feet and toes. I sat in the middle and grabbed the champagne glass.

"I know I should give him a chance, but I just feel like the Asha chick is doing too much," I fussed, gulping the rest of the drink.

"It's his job to get rid of her, not yours." Maya leaned over and picked out the color of their nails.

"You're right."

"Exactly, you have to remember Jordan has changed from the bachelor he used to be. I promise, you have my brother wrapped around your finger," Chelsey reminded me. I thought about his devious smile whenever he wanted to fuck, and the way his smooth hands rubbed against my large breasts. His six-pack abs and thick thighs were the first things I fell in love with. The bulge in his pants when I drove us back from the airport had my mind going crazy. Plus, his scent drew me in even though he was arrogant and charming at the same time.

"All right, I'll let him run the show tonight, but if I see Asha again, I need you to make sure you get me out on bail."

Maya laughed and slapped hands with me.

CHAPTER 4

JORDAN

Xavier lifted the beer and tossed his head back in laughter. I came to his house to let off some steam after we played ball in the backyard with Warren and Mason. The girls went to the spa, and that gave me time to get things in order for my night with Emma. Asha tried to call me nonstop after I had one of my business managers contact her about leading the renovations. He told me she was pissed and cursed him out because I let my wife carry the balls. At first, I wanted to call her back, but the fellas said it would be pointless, and I agreed.

"So, what are you doing tonight?" Warren opened another beer.

"I reserved a room at the club. It's been a while." I picked up a slice of pizza.

"Emma knows you reserved it tonight?" Xavier tossed his napkin in the trash.

"No, I mean she is getting ready for a date tonight. I had her get her nails and shit done."

"You better eat a lot of pussy, man," Xavier joked, and I chuckled.

"Shit, who are you telling? That's my baby though."

"You started all this when you didn't get rid of Asha," Mason reminded me.

"Here he goes." I burped and sat back in the chair.

"He's right. I never let a woman even get a hint that something is going to happen," Warren informed me.

"True, and I never let her down. Asha's just spoiled."

"Hopefully, you set her straight." Xavier flipped open the box of meat lover's pizza.

"The client account was switched to another bank manager."

"Good, you had Chelsey pissed at me," Xavier hinted.

"What the fuck? Why?"

"You know those girls stick together," Xavier said.

"Emma knows I've never cheated. She's the only woman for me."

"But are you consistent in showing her?" Mason brought up.

I rubbed my chin, thinking over the past few weeks and months. Emma did bring up that I worked a lot more and skipped out on events.

"You got me there." I threw my hands up in surrender.

"Tonight, make it all about her." Mason washed his hands and opened a bottle of water.

"Anything else I should do to get out of the doghouse?"

"Eat a lot of pussy," they said at the same time. We burst into laughter.

* * *

EMMA HAD a car pick her up and bring her to me, and I held my breath and prayed we would make a step forward after tonight. I didn't see her when she came home, but I left instructions for her to put on a dress I had delivered.

Once lunch was over with the guys, I came here to the club, showered, and helped to set things in motion. The Red Room—or VIP, as they liked to call it—was opulently decorated with its own bathroom, fireplace, TV, and living room, separate from the bedroom. All of the toys would be used tonight, and I made a commitment to keep us locked until we both agreed to keep better communication open moving forward.

Knock! Knock!

I checked myself out in the mirror and brushed my waves again. I wore a black silk robe and pants to match her black dress. I opened the door, and her beauty blew my breath away. She peered at me with a grin on her face, and I reached a hand out for her to come inside.

"Damn, baby."

"You picked this out." She ran a hand down the silky black dress with spaghetti straps. Her full figure had my dick hard as a rock. The way her breasts filled the bodice and the extra weight on her ass after having my son, forced my mind into dirty places.

"What do you have up your sleeve?" She walked around the room in awe.

I came up behind her and lifted her off her feet.

"Jordan, put me down!" She screamed in laughter, and I chuckled.

I laid her on the bed, pushed my legs between hers, and hovered over her chest. Emma's breathing heightened, and her eyes locked on mine.

"You love me?"

"Yes."

"Say it."

I love you."

"I promise tonight is about us, and no one can take your place."

"Not even Asha?" she teased, and I slid my hand up her chest to pull down a strap on her gown. I did the same thing to her right breast and licked my lips.

"Asha who?" I asked.

"Good answer."

She tried to reach up and pull me on top of her, but I moved back. She pouted.

"Stop playing, Jordan."

"You stop playing. We haven't done this in a while. You remember the safeword?"

"I do and what about you?" Her brow hiked in suspicion.

"Fuck, yes." I picked up the oil on the side of the bed and brought it closer to me.

"So, what is the safeword for tonight?"

"Blue, and all you need to do is relax and let me handle you."

"Handle soft or hard?"

"Both." I sucked her bottom lip, squeezing her right thigh.

She moaned and tried to arch into me.

"Can we do some nipple play tonight?" I questioned.

"Yesss…" she cooed, squeezing her breasts together.

I removed my robe and grabbed the clamps and oil. She watched me climb back on the bed. I caressed her cheek, moved my hand over her right breast, and licked her nipple.

"Ohhh… Jordan."

"Love when you're responsive, baby."

I rubbed some oil between her breasts, down her arms, then her legs. Then I rubbed her lower lips and watched her facial expressions as I put clamps on each nipple.

"How was the massage today?"

"Goodddd," she dragged out.

I stared at both clamps and then ripped her dress in half.

"Ugh, Jordan!" I slid a finger in and out of her pussy.

She arched her back, as my tongue locked on her nipples.

"You taste so good, baby."

"Fuck me!" she cried out.

"Not yet."

Emma wound her hips and tried to stick her hand inside her pussy, but I slapped it away.

My stiffness was ready to pound her for trying to take charge of what I had planned.

"Please, can I... arghh."

I stuck my tongue in her pussy and latched onto her clit.

I used my left hand to rub her breast. She shook underneath my hold, and I was ready to slide in and give her what she wanted. I pulled back, and her head popped up in anger. I smirked.

"What are you doing?"

"Before we go any further, I need you to swear that you'll never get an idea of me stepping out on you again."

"Jordan, this is not the time to bring something like that up."

"Actually, it's the perfect time."

I stroked my dick and waited for her answer.

She cut her eyes at me.

"Jordan."

"Come on, answer the question."

I tapped the head against her essence.

"Yes, Jordan. You feel so good," she purred

"That's not the question."

She squeezed her eyes shut and bit her bottom lip when I slid just the tip in and didn't move.

"Okay, baby, I swear. No more foolish thoughts. I trust you."

Her breasts heaved up and down. I thrusted, slamming my lips on hers. Our moans of pleasure emitted when our skin clapped together.

I placed my hands on her waist and watched my dick disappear. The night was still early, but the way she gripped me around my pole had me biting my tongue.

The bed shook, and I moved in long strokes for the next few minutes before I pulled out and switched places with her.

"We aren't leaving this room, so prepare to ride my face, baby." I lay on the bed and tapped her thigh to get up, and she sluggishly rose and crawled on top of me. She held on tight to the headboard, and I eased my tongue inside, with my finger in her asshole.

"Ooh, shit…" she groaned.

Hours later, we had used most of the toys, from the cock ring to the floggers and a swing. I stared at her beautiful face as she slept peacefully next to me.

CHAPTER 5

JORDAN

A month later, conversation flowed at the dinner table with my parents. They wanted us to join them along with a few of our friends for dinner. Normally, family dinner would be just us and the kids. Maya was high-profile, and my parents loved the attention when she came to visit. News reporters would put our family in the paper when she showed up. Emma rubbed my thigh under the table, and I placed my hand on hers as we ate. Jr. sat in the high chair next to me while I fed him off my plate.

"How is the senate going for you, Maya?" my father asked.

Maya picked up her glass of water and took a sip.

"Fine, just busy with trying to push bills through and balance married life." She chuckled.

"Back in my day, all we had to do was stay home with the kids. Women nowadays, I give them praise with how much pressure they have," Mom said.

That was funny coming from her because she didn't feel like Xavier was good enough for Chelsey since he didn't come from money. She'd evolved over the past few years now that we had kids; it made her see the world differently.

"Some women," my dad said and glared at Emma.

He found out Asha and I weren't working on the project together because of Emma's concerns. Her father talked to my dad about the situation, and he was pissed with me for letting a woman run me. I told him we respected each other when something made us uncomfortable, and Asha flirted too much for my liking, but he didn't care.

"Mr. Hayden," Emma started to say, but I shook my head.

"Pops, it's over. We still have the deal. She just has another person handling it as a point of contact."

"Our reputation is a big deal, Jordan. You shouldn't let anything confuse that," he spat.

"Daddy!" Chelsey shouted.

"It's okay, Chelsey." Emma clasped her hands together.

"Chelsey, stay out of this."

"Mr. Hayden, we've never had an issue, and I respect you as a grandfather to my son, but please stay out of my marriage."

He scoffed and marched out of the room. My mother jumped up and followed him.

"I like that shit," I whispered in her ear.

"What shit?"

"You being a badass."

Emma laid her hand on the back of my neck and kissed me. Dinner continued without my parents, so we decided to head out to a bar together. My dad apologized to Emma and agreed to let our son stay the night.

* * *

EMMA BENT over and grabbed her ankles, popping her hips with me behind her on the dance floor. It was like we were young and in love after the other night together. All we did was replay the events at the club and her screams all night as I thrusted inside her. I hoped to have her pregnant again.

"Let me see how low you can go." I smacked her on the ass, and she twerked before rising up. I laid a hand on her stomach and pulled her back to my chest.

"You look sexy tonight."

"Can't wait to take you home."

"Take me home and do what?"

"Suck your dick." She whirled around, extended her hand out, and we slowed to dance to an old Keith Sweat song.

"I want you forever. I want more babies."

"The crazy part is I want the same thing."

"Glad you didn't let my father push you away."

The music changed, and I escorted her back to our booth with the rest of the couples.

Chelsey sat on Xavier's lap. Maya couldn't come because of her job, so they went home, but Kyra came with Warren.

"Did you film today?" Emma hugged Kyra.

"Yes, it was a long shoot," Kyra complained. I hugged her, and we sat down.

"Baby, what do you want to drink?" I rubbed her back, and the bottle girl approached our section to take her order.

"A bottle of Jack." Emma fidgeted in her seat.

"Can she get a Jack, and I'll have a cognac?"

The DJ played the latest from Lizzo, and I scanned the crowd as my eyes caught an annoying face. Asha watched us from the bar, and I chuckled when she rolled her eyes at me.

"What's funny?" Emma asked.

"Some people can't take a hint." I pointed at Asha.

Emma glanced around the crowd and saw Asha with some girls and started to jump up.

"That bitch!" Emma shouted, and I grabbed her hand.

"Sit down. She's not worth a fight."

"Like hell she ain't."

"Emma, the girl is bitter and jealous. Calm down because you are a queen and never have to stoop to her level."

She relaxed, sat back down on my lap, and turned to straddle my lap. I laughed at her antics.

"You're petty."

"Call me Petty Betty, because she's going to learn." Emma forced her tongue down in my mouth.

"Hmmmmh," she moaned.

We danced and drank for the next hour before going home.

CHAPTER 6

EMMA

"*D*o you like my new hair color?" Jordan closed his eyes tight and growled his pleasure. I was in control after the other night at the club and felt his big hands rub against my ass. I knew I needed another session in the playroom. Right now, I had his balls in my mouth, and I popped them out as he grabbed the back of my head.

"Stop playing, baby."

I scraped my nails against his thighs and made eye contact with him.

"Shut up." I popped his dick back in my mouth, moved up and down, gagged a little like he liked, and fondled with my breasts.

I rose off the bed and grabbed the beads then oil and got in position. Took a small amount in my hand rubbed across my ass, plus the beads.

"Fuck me on my side, baby." He grabbed the beads out of my hands, ran the oil along my pussy, asshole, and kissed both cheeks. I threw my head back in pleasure.

"Arghhh, Jordan! Baby, keep going."

My essence covered the bed, as he stuck the beads in his mouth, pushed them up to mine, and slowly eased through the barrier.

"Ummm. God." I felt my body tremble. His dick slowly pushed home.

His balls slapped against my skin. I reached up and gripped the pillow. Jordan gasped, then lifted my leg a little higher and went deeper.

"Damn, I love you, Emma."

Roughly cuffing my breasts with his other hand and thrusting faster, I felt my orgasm rise and my vision get blurry.

"Emma! Fuckkkk, I'm about to explode."

"Me too!"

Jordan pushed me onto my stomach and hammered me as I convulsed from my orgasm. He came and fell on top of me, kissing down my back. He rolled off to the side of the bed.

"That was amazing." We tried to catch our breaths.

"Sinful, you know that."

I giggled and turned my head toward him.

"I bring that side out of you, huh?" He grasped my hand and kissed my fingernails one by one.

"I'd do anything for you. Just never leave me, baby."

"I'd never do that."

"Let's head to the shower, and then we can watch a show." He reminded me of the scene with one of the couples we liked to watch when they had sex. They loved the public to watch them, and it turned Jordan on even more. We would probably come back to the room afterwards and go another round in bed.

* * *

CHELSEY PARKED BEHIND US, and I unlocked my seat belt and slid out of the car while Jordan helped Jr. out of his car seat. Today, we reserved the kids' playhouse for the next three hours and brought all of our kids. Maya and Mason were right behind us, as I pulled the door open and looked around at all of the play sections for each child range. Jordan and I held hands and headed to the front counter. They pointed to the section we could start with as I paid for the coins they use.

"Are you ready to go play, baby?" Jr. clapped his hands in excitement, wiggling to get out of his father's arms.

"Watch him while I get us something to drink," Jordan said, walking to the food counter.

Maya and Chelsey helped the kids on the playpen. I laughed at Jr.'s giggling and throwing balls back at the other kids.

"You seem chipper today?" Chelsey nudged me in the arm.

"Feel good, and my baby is happy."

"Probably has to do with you and my brother joined at the hip."

Chelsey's booty bumped me. I lifted my shoulders in a shrug.

"Look at Jr. help the girls climb out." I pointed. He was already a gentleman.

"My nephew is already cute. Wait until he turns sixteen."

"Please don't remind me."

"I talked with Mason about our baby growing up. He's already talking about keeping a gun ready." Maya chortled.

"I hope you reminded him that you're the senator in Memphis. He can't go around threatening people."

We watched the kids laugh and enjoy themselves

together. Jordan planted his arm around my shoulder and winked.

"I was thinking…"

"About?"

"We renew our vows."

I jerked back in surprise.

"Huh?"

"The guys and I talked. We think that maybe in a few months, we do a little vow renewal and a getaway trip."

"Are you my Jordan, or did someone kidnap your body?" I ran my hand across his forehead, and he laughed.

"All me, baby. No, seriously, you scared me there for a while, and that got me into a different headspace."

"Like where is this going?"

"Maybe with my parents, we do something that's just close friends and family, but I want to take you away first."

"Did you forget about our son?" I pointed in the direction of Jr. playing in the train station with Xavier.

"Chelsey and Xavier are willing to keep him for a few days."

"Since you have all the answers, I can't say no to you."

"Perfect. I can't wait to get you alone."

"Same, honey."

Finally, we had peace and quiet in the house. After all the kids ran around at the playhouse, they didn't want to leave each other, so we took them for ice cream. I rubbed the lotion on my hands and lifted the scarf over my hair. Jordan lay in bed with a book, and the game played on the TV. I slipped under the covers in a t-shirt and panties and pulled his free arm around my waist. I yawned, picked up the remote, and switched through channels.

"Tired?"

"Kids wore me out today." I placed a hand on his chest.

Jordan closed his book and focused on me with his back against the headboard.

"I'm serious about us renewing our vows."

"I believe you."

"Tell the truth. How close were you to kicking my ass out of the house?"

"Very close, and a possible stepdaddy on speed dial," I joked while he bombarded me with tickles.

"Sorry, stop! Jordan, sorry." I laughed for a long time, until tears gathered in my eyes.

"Maybe I should go find Asha."

I slapped his chest.

"Get cursed out."

He gripped my chin, pushed me on my back, and sucked on my neck. I raised my arms around his waist and inhaled the warmth of his body against mine.

"Trust me, she's not in your league," he remarked, and I felt him ease his dick in slowly, and we made love for the rest of the night.

EPILOGUE

JORDAN

The pilot explained we needed to put our seat belts on as we were prepared to land. I picked up her hand, kissed the back of her palm, and relaxed my eyes. Our trip was planned without her knowing any of the details, and she was completely surprised when we drove to the landing strip. Our family's private jet flew us to Costa Rica, and we rented out an entire villa for just the two of us. Chelsey didn't hesitate to watch our son. A few seconds later after we stepped off the plane and loaded in the limo with our bags, the driver headed to our villa.

"Baby, this is beautiful."

I pulled her to my chest.

"You deserve it, baby."

She poked her lips up, and I cupped her chin, peppering her with kisses.

We drove through the streets, and I pointed to different landmarks I'd love to visit.

"I'm starving."

"Lunch is being served on the beach. We'll get there, unload our bags, and change."

"You're in the running for best husband of the year with this vacation." Emma removed her phone and took photos.

"I'm working on husband of the lifetime." I grinned. When the car arrived at the villa, the driver put in the code and drove to the entrance. The place was over twenty thousand square feet, with a pool, a private beach, basketball court, and a theater. Our driver opened the passenger door, and I helped Emma to step out, and he grabbed our bags. The butler and house manager opened the front door. I shook hands with them, and Emma scanned the high ceilings.

"This is incredible, Jordan." Emma walked to the double stairs in the front, turned to the open-space living room, then she found the kitchen.

"Baby, we should shower and change for lunch."

"Welcome again, Mr. and Mrs. Hayden," the house manager said.

"Thank you. We're excited to be here." Emma hugged her, and I grasped her hand. We started upstairs to our room. Emma released my hand and ran to the double doors of the balcony. I removed my jacket and lay on the bed.

She came over to me and straddled my lap.

"I'm going to have to reward you for our trip."

I grinned and planted my hands on her thighs.

"I have ideas."

Emma bent down and buried her face in my neck. I groaned and slid a hand up her back to grip her neck.

"We have lunch, baby."

She slid her hand down to my chest.

"Thank you for making us a priority." She interlocked our hands.

"Thank you for not giving up on me. Promise, you come first."

"First lunch, then I want my dessert with you naked on the bed." She brushed her lips across mine, and I gripped her hands tighter.

"Fuck lunch."

Emma giggled, and we stayed like that for the next hour or two.

BONUS SCENE

EMMA

Six months later.

"Taste this." I slid some strawberry cheesecake in his mouth, and he smashed his lips to mine. Today was our anniversary dinner with our friends and family. Earlier, we had a small ceremony and renewed our vows. Most of the food was catered except the dessert that I handmade because he loved only the cheesecake that I made. I wiped remnants of my lipstick away from his lip and pulled back to the cheers of our friends and family.

"Congrats again, Emma and Jordan. You both look so happy." Kadence leaned in to hug me, then Jordan.

"Thank you, Kadence. Is Kyrin having fun?" I peered over to the table she sat on. Now a single mom, she was still dealing with grief. At first, she didn't want to come. It would have been too much for her with the death of her husband.

"Kyrin was happy the minute he saw the dessert table." She laughed, and we watched him eat a piece of cake with some other kids his age.

"Don't forget if you're still looking for a job to let me know."

"Thanks, I will. Still waiting on a few interviews to come back."

"Kadence, do you mind if I steal my bride for a dance?" Jordan grasped my hand.

"Go enjoy. We'll talk soon."

"Come on, wife. They're playing our song."

The DJ played an old-school ballad from the sixties. Jordan knew I loved old R&B that really told a story of a guy and girl in love. We swayed on the dance floor in my in-laws' backyard and grinned as he licked his lips.

"How does it feel?" he asked.

"How does what feel?"

"To have me so deeply in love with you, I would walk through fire to make you happy."

"I would walk through fire to make you happy." We rubbed our noses together.

"I got lucky." Jordan placed both hands around my lower back. We didn't do anything traditional, from my red strapless cocktail dress to only including our closest family and friends, to serving a barbeque buffet, and Jr. standing as his father's best man. Our route after six years had shown me more love, devotion, and trust in the people we'd become through the storm.

"How about we slip out of here and head to the club?" Jordan trailed kisses down my neck, lifted my hand, and caressed my palm.

"You remember your safeword?"

He groaned, lightly biting my neck, and I felt his dick get hard between us.

"Fuck the club. We can go upstairs to my old bedroom," he said, and we burst into laughter.

* * *

I hope you enjoyed Emma and Jordan's story. Please also check out Kadence and Gunner in **"Seek to Earn"** here https://books2read.com/u/bPgyRz

Don't forget if you love Fling romances, bodyguard, forced proximity then check out, **"Protecting Chanel"** https://books2read.com/u/mqwPB8

If you love brother's best friend romance, then you'll love **"Sensual" here** https://books2read.com/u/49lYYM with a dash of steamy romance.

Check out Bodyguard Romance, military, romantic suspense here *"Protecting Bria"* https://books2read.com/u/bQJkjd

Another military romance, suspense that features familiar characters is "Protecting Chanel" here https://books2read.com/u/mqwPB8

How about a steamy, medical romance? Check out *"Haven"* https://books2read.com/u/4jAvyZ a steamy enemies to lovers romance.

Have you checked out **"His Peace Her Pleasure"**? Click here https://books2read.com/u/3JJr0P a billionaire, steamy romance.

Please also check out my *"Love Don't Live here Anymore"* https://books2read.com/u/mBOWGZ a steamy enemies to lovers romance.

SNEAK PEEK PROTECTING YANIRA

SPECIAL FORCES OPERATION

Yanira ~

As a journalist, I need to remain objective, but that doesn't mean I don't have opinions. When I find my boss dead in the office, I'm more determined than ever to find answers. But my investigation leads me down dangerous territory and exposes a threat that's too close to home.

Bishop ~

A night out with friends sometimes comes with surprises, but when a woman literally lands in my arms, that's only the beginning of what will be the biggest surprise of my life. She's in trouble and I know what to do to keep trouble at bay. But it would be a whole lot easier if the woman wasn't as bossy and uptight as she is beautiful and irresistible.

Will the sexual tension help or hinder the search for the killer?

ABOUT THE AUTHOR

A Tennessee native and CA dreaming Author Keke Renee is living and striving to continue her passion of writing Short Story romances from Erotic, Women's Fiction, Romantic Suspense, Paranormal and Urban fiction.

304 PUBLISHING COMPANY

WE SHOWCASE AUTHORS WRITING African American, Interracial, Women's Fiction, Urban Romance, Erotic, and Contemporary Romance novels. Along with Thriller, Suspense, Poetry, Beauty, and Style Books. Thank you for taking the time out to visit. Join our mailing list to stay updated with new releases and blog posts.

WHAT'S NEXT

WANT TO KNOW WHAT happens next?

Follow me on Bookbub and social media today.

Reviews are the lifeblood of the publishing world. They're read, appreciated, and needed. Please consider taking the time to leave a few words on wherever you buy books. Sign up for updates and sneak peeks at the site below.

CATALOG OF RELEASES BY KEKE RENÉE:

Catalog of Releases By Keke Renée:
- Wet Heat (Wet Heat Series Book 1)
- Every Time We Touch Novelette (Wet Heat Book 2 Series)
- His Peace, Her Pleasure
- Baby, It's Cold Outside
- Love Don't Live Here Anymore, Vanessa Andrew Book 1
- Love Don't Live Here Anymore, Isabella Andrew Book2
- One Night Only-A Novelette (Love By Design Book 1)
- Cassian and Savannah (Love By Design Book 2)
- Deidra's Love (Love By Design Book 3)
- Protecting Bria (Special Force Operation Alphas)

Thank you so much for reading, and if you enjoyed the crazy ride and decide to leave a review we'd truly appreciate the support.

www.ingramcontent.com/pod-product-compliance
Lightning Source LLC
Chambersburg PA
CBHW021319160726
47994CB00004B/1518